Madeline Finn
and the
Shelter Dog

To all the Miss Ivys of the world—you know who you are—thank you.
The work you do, the love you share, makes the world a better place.

—L. P.

Published by
Peachtree Publishers
1700 Chattahoochee Avenue
Atlanta, Georgia 30318-2112
www.peachtree-online.com

Text and illustrations © 2019 by Lisa Papp

Edited by Kathy Landwehr
Design by Lisa Papp and Nicola Simmonds Carmack
Composition by Nicola Simmonds Carmack
The illustrations were rendered in pencil and paper, with watercolor and digital coloring.

Printed in September 2018 by Tien Wah Press, Malaysia
10 9 8 7 6 5 4 3 2 1
First Edition
ISBN 978-1-68263-075-4

Library of Congress Cataloging-in-Publication Data

Names: Papp, Lisa, author, illustrator.
Title: Madeline Finn and the shelter dog / Lisa Papp.
Description: Atlanta : Peachtree Publishers, [2019] | Summary: When Madeline Finn learns about animal shelters, she wants to do something to make the residents feel loved.
Identifiers: LCCN 2018003496 | ISBN 9781682630754
Subjects: | CYAC: Animal shelters—Fiction. | Dogs—Fiction.
Classification: LCC PZ7.P2116 Md 2019 | DDC [E]—dc23 LC record available at *https://lccn.loc.gov/2018003496*

Madeline Finn
and the
Shelter Dog

Lisa Papp

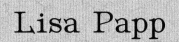

PEACHTREE
ATLANTA

I ask Mom every single day.

In the morning.   In the evening.

Even when we're out.

And finally, she says yes!

"Hello, Madeline Finn," Mrs. Dimple says when we arrive. "Your mom says you're ready to pick out one of Bonnie's puppies."

"Yes, please," I say. But first, I give Bonnie a big hug. "Hi, Bonnie!"

I'm so excited, I can't decide which puppy to choose. "I love them all," I tell Mom.

"Why don't you see if someone picks you?" Mrs. Dimple asks.

So I close my eyes and think of the name I picked for my puppy.

"Star," I whisper, and the littlest one crawls right into my lap!

woof, he says, real soft.

"It worked!" I say. "Is this how you chose Bonnie?"

"Not quite," Mrs. Dimple says. "There are lots of ways to find animals. Do you know what a shelter is?"

I look at Mom.

"A shelter is a place where animals wait for good homes," she says.

"Like a hotel?" I ask.

"Sort of," Mrs. Dimple says. "Except the animals want homes where they can stay forever. They need forever homes."

"How many animals are there?" I ask. "Do they have snakes?"

"It's not a zoo," Mrs. Dimple explains. "But there are lots of dogs and cats. I volunteer at the shelter. Bonnie comes too. Why don't you join us sometime?"

"Can we, Mom?" I ask.

"We'd love to," Mom says.

Before we go, Mrs. Dimple says, "Madeline Finn,
you have a new job now, with lots of responsibilities."
Then she tells me everything I need to do, like walking
Star, and feeding him, and making sure he has a safe
place to sleep.

"But the most important thing," she says, "is love."

"I love you, Star," I say when
  I feed him.

"I love you, Star," I say when
  I read to him.

"I love you, Star," I say when
  I tuck him in.

"It's okay, Star," I say when he
  has an accident on the floor.

"I love you."

On Saturday, Mrs. Dimple invites us to the shelter.

"Thank you for the donations," a lady tells Mrs. Dimple.

Then she smiles at me. "My name is Miss Ivy. Would you like

to meet some of our animals?"

"Yes, please," I say.

"Hi," I say to the first dog I see, but he doesn't even wag his tail. The sign on his cage says his name is Mr. Chips.

We meet lots of dogs. And cats. And even some bunnies and birds.

"They all need homes?" I ask.

Miss Ivy nods. She seems a little sad.

I think Mr. Chips is sad too.

"Mom," I ask when we get home, "do shelter dogs

get to play outside?"

"Probably not as much as Star," she says.

"Do shelter dogs get to sleep under blankets?"

"I'm not sure, honey."

"Mrs. Dimple said love was most important," I say.

"That's right, dear."

"Mom…does anyone tell the shelter dogs they love them?"

Mom is quiet. Then she gives me a big hug.

"Maybe you can show them."

The next day, I rummage through our linen closet. "The sign at the shelter said they need towels," I say. "Can we bring some?"

"I bet they would like that," Mom says.

Miss Ivy is happy to see us. "Thank you, Madeline Finn,"
she says. "These will make soft beds for the animals."

But when we leave, I notice there weren't enough towels for
all the animals.

And Mr. Chips still looks sad.

Before bed, I practice reading to Star.

Then I whisper in his ear, "I love you, Star."

woof, he says, real soft.

When Mom tucks us in, I say, "Star loves

when I read to him."

"He sure does, sweetie."

"Mom?"

"Yes, dear?"

"Does anyone read to the shelter dogs?"

In the morning, we talk with Mrs. Dimple about my new idea.

Then Star and I spend all week collecting towels and blankets

from the neighbors.

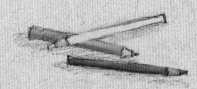

I make special signs and Mrs. Dimple helps me hang them in the library.

Saturday 10:00

Come read to the shelter animals.

Bring a blanket and a book.

On Friday night, I barely sleep I'm so excited.

When Saturday comes, I'm ready. So is Star!

But when we arrive, it's just us.

"Nobody else came," I tell Star.

woof, he says real soft.

"I'm glad you're here," Miss Ivy says when I hand her the blankets and towels. "Why don't you get started?"

I sit by the first dog. We're both a little nervous. But when I start reading, she wags her tail.

The next dog perks up his ears when I read to him.

Even the cats around the corner are listening.

But after my fifth story, I'm *still* the only one here.

"I don't have enough books," I tell Miss Ivy. "Or enough blankets."

"I know, Madeline Finn," she says, "I know."

Then I hear footsteps…

Bonnie comes first.

Behind her are lots of kids with lots of books and lots
of blankets.

"Sorry we're late," I hear a parent say. "There was a
crowd at the library checking out books."

Miss Ivy shows everyone how to sit with the
dogs and read to them.

Pretty soon, the shelter looks like a library!

"Did everyone get a story?" I ask Mom.

"I think so, sweetie."

"And a blanket?"

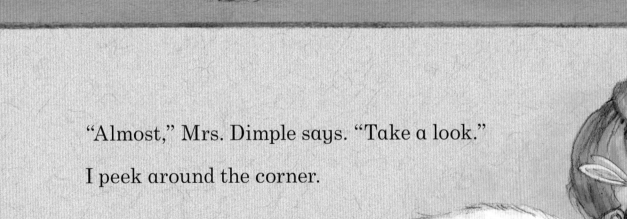

"Almost," Mrs. Dimple says. "Take a look."

I peek around the corner.

Mr. Chips didn't

get a blanket...

…he was going home in one!

"Mr. Chips found a new family today," Mrs. Dimple says.

"He's getting a real home," Mom says.

"A *forever* home," I say.

And Star lets out a giant *WOOF!*